ten heads for tanuj

PRIYA NARAYANAN

ILLUSTRATED
by
SHAMIKA
CHAVES

HarperCollins*Children'sBooks*

First published in India in 2018 by HarperCollins Children's Books
An imprint of HarperCollins *Publishers*

HarperCollins Publishers India, Cyber City, Building 10-A, Gurugram,
Haryana-122002, India
www.harpercollins.co.in

2 4 6 8 10 9 7 5 3 1

P-ISBN: 978-93-5302-350-8

Typeset in Helvetica Neue Regular 14pt/ 18
by Shamika Chaves, Mumbai, India

Printed and bound at MicroPrints India, New Delhi

FSC MIX Paper FSC™ C218906

This product is made of FSC®-certified and other controlled material.

HarperCollins Publishers, Macken House, 39/40 Mayor Street
Upper, Dublin 1, D01 C9W8, Ireland

1

The city had recently celebrated Dussehra with great fervour. The memory of the burning effigies of Ravana, Meghnad and Kumbhakarna was fresh in nine-year-old Tanuj's mind. As the sound of claps and hoots filled the air, the ten heads of Ravana had tumbled to the ground in a cloud of smoke.

One night soon after, Tanuj clambered on to bed and snuggled next to Amma to listen to his favourite bedtime story.

'Ravana was the greatest of all Asura Kings,' began Amma with the pomp of a true storyteller. She narrated the story of the ten-headed devotee of Lord Shiva, who was both a hero and a villain. 'He was so strong, he once lifted the entire Mount Kailasa with his hands. And his ten heads were not really heads but a symbol of his knowledge of the four Vedas and six Upanishads,' she added.

Although he had heard it innumerable times before—145 to be precise—Tanuj was spellbound by the time Amma finished her story. 'East or West, Ravana is the Best,' he mumbled over and over again, before falling asleep.

When Tanuj opened his eyes the next morning, his head felt as heavy as a rock as he tried to lift it off the pillow. 'What is wrong with me?' he wondered. When, after five failed attempts, he finally stood up straight and wobbled to the mirror, he let out a piercing shriek, 'Aaaaaaaaaah!'

Amma dashed upstairs, worried, and before one could say T for Trouble, she fell in a faint.

Appa's brains were bamboozled. A giant scream rushed up his throat, but he bravely choked it midway. 'What did you do, Tanuj?' he squeaked.

'I don't know! All I did was dream of Ravana after Amma narrated his story last night!' replied Tanuj, pointing an accusing finger at his mother.

Appa glared at Amma, who had managed to get back to her feet after he made her smell Tanuj's stinky socks.

'What?' she said in self-defence. 'That's the only story I know!'

Appa sighed. 'So Tanuj has ten heads now,' he mumbled, 'that means ten sets of teeth to be brushed. No problem. I'll run to the grocer's and get nine more toothbrushes. Then we'll be all set.'

Appa's mind was in a boggle as he hurried to the grocer. When he returned, he found Amma wiping the tears off ten pairs of cheeks. She wrung the soaking wet handkerchief into a bucket before getting down to brush the teeth on five of Tanuj's brand new heads.

Appa did the same on the remaining five.

2

There was gloom in the room with Tanuj fumbling and tumbling as he got ready for school. For all her bewilderment, Amma wasn't one to allow him to miss school. For if Tanuj missed school, he'd lose the 'Highest Attendance' award to Rohan, and she'd lose the bet she'd made with Rohan's mother. So, she busied herself helping him with the uniform and socks. When it was time to comb his hair, Appa and Amma divided the task once again.

'Hey, look at the bright side,' Appa tried to sound chirpy as his pocket comb slid over the slick black hair on one of Tanuj's heads. 'You can have a different hairstyle on each of your heads; that makes for ten different styles! So cool, right?'

However, hairstyle was the last thing on Tanuj's mind. Silent as a stone, he hung his glum heads and plodded out, walking sideways to get himself through the door.

Soon, the school bus announced itself with an annoying honk. Peering out of the window, Tanuj saw the yellow bus and began to wail. 'I cannot go to school like this!'

'Yes, he cannot!' agreed Appa.

But Amma was not sure. She furrowed her brows and scratched her head. It wasn't a good idea to lose the bet with Rohan's mother. But neither was sending Tanuj to school. And so, for better or for worse, she decided that Tanuj would stay at home until they could find a solution to his predicament.

On his first day at home, Tanuj watched Amma fumbling with the vessels in the kitchen. 'How will one bowl of upma suffice for a boy with ten heads?' she said, worriedly.

‘I have ten heads, Ma, but only one stomach,’ Tanuj replied. Then, as Amma looked on wide-eyed, he polished off all the upma in under a minute, his ten mouths working like a machine. For the rest of the day, he walked up and down his room to get his balance right.

On the second day, Tanuj helped Appa join his bed with the spare bed from the guest room. And he helped Amma dig out all the extra pillows from the attic and arrange them neatly on the extended bed.

On the third day, Tanuj tried everything he could to get rid of the extra heads. He tried to pull them out. He tried to knock them down. And he tried to make a magic balm to rub on his heads and make them disappear. But nothing worked.

That night, a big yawn escaped each of his mouths as he devoured a bowl of noodles for dinner. As soon as his heads sank into the pillows, he drifted off to sleep.

3

'You don't seem happy with your new heads,' a voice boomed into Tanuj's ears, making him toss and turn in his sleep.

'Err ... Umm ... Uh,' Tanuj stammered, startled by the sudden appearance of the great Ravana himself. 'Well, it's rather uncomfortable to walk around with ten heads,' he tried to reason.

'But you're the one who
wished for them!'

'No, I didn't,' Tanuj said, crossing his arms. 'I don't mean any offence, but I'd NEVER wish for ten heads. They look quite silly and ...'

'SILLY! Did you just say that I, the King of all Asura Kings, look SILLY?' Ravana thundered.

'Yes ... I mean n ... n ... no!' Tanuj said, taken aback by Ravana's sudden anger. 'You do not look silly at all. I am the one looking silly. After all, one does need a strong personality like yours to carry off this style and I, sadly, do not have that,' he stammered and stumbled, trying to appease the Asura King.

‘Now THAT is true,’ Ravana said, twirling the edges of his fine black moustache. ‘No one in this whole wide world, not even Rama, has my charisma. Why else did he have only one head on his otherwise strong pair of shoulders, huh?’

‘Y … yes, of course! Even Rama did not have your personality, O Mighty King, and neither do I. I do not even have the strength to carry these heads everywhere I go. My limbs have gone weak and my knees are about to give way! Please tell me how I can get rid of them. In return, I’ll do anything you say.’

‘That’s interesting,’ Ravana remarked. ‘So, you’re willing to do anything to get rid of the extra heads?’

‘Yes, of course ... ANYTHING!’

‘Hmmm ...’ Ravana pondered. Just then, his eyes fell on the rows of medals and trophies decorating Tanuj’s shelf. ‘What are these for?’ he asked. ‘Do humans also wear fancy necklaces and drink from golden cups?’

‘No. What a curious thing to do!’ Tanuj replied. Then, with his voice dripping with pride, he said, ‘These are proof that I’m the smartest in my class. I’ve won many competitions and have been the class topper since I was in class 1, you know?’

‘Hah! How can anyone be the class topper when I, the great Ravana, am the most intelligent of all. Didn't you pay attention to your mother's story?' Ravana snarled. He closed his eyes for a while and scratched his forehead, as though thinking about something. When he opened them again, they were red with anger. 'Prove to me that YOU are not as intelligent as I am, and I will rid you of your heads,' he roared.

Tanuj tried not to panic. 'Oh, that should be easy,' he said. 'Go on, ask me any question and I shall give only the wrongest of answers.' Then, before Ravana could say anything, he continued, 'Did you notice that 'wrongest' in itself is a wrong word to use? You see, I'm already proving to be way less than intelligent!'

'Not so soon, my lad,' Ravana interrupted. 'To prove that you are not as intelligent as I am, you must fail in your upcoming exams at school.' A vile toothy grin appeared on each of his ten heads, as he slapped his thighs.

'Wh ... WHAT? FAIL in my exams? Impossible! I cannot fail … I'm the class topper and in the running for the Best Student Award! No no no … can't I just score low marks?' Tanuj sank to his knees and pleaded with folded hands.

But Ravana was not one to budge. 'No. Don't be chicken and rise up to the challenge!' he said, turning his heads the other way.

Tanuj was in despair as he realized that the only way the Asura King would give in was if he failed his exams. Nevertheless, he decided to give it one last try.

'Can I fail in only one subject then? My parents will be devastated if I fail in all the subjects. You would know the importance of keeping one's parents happy …'

'Umm … ahem … yes, yes, of course,' Ravana replied, flustered. He did love his parents and had been a dutiful son to them despite being a bit arrogant at times. Maybe it wasn't entirely fair to make Tanuj's parents pay for his troubles. Getting off the throne, he swung his angavastram over his shoulder dramatically and said, ‘Fine, you can fail in only one subject then. But the subject will be of my choosing ... and I choose MATHS!’

Tanuj felt weak at the knees, and his head started to spin. Maths was his favourite. Miss Mohanty said he had a natural flair for it. It would be a Kumbhakarnesque task to fail in Maths! But there was no escape now, because Ravana had vanished. POOF!

4

The next morning, Tanuj announced that he would be going to school. He wasn't sure he should listen to the Ravana of his dreams, and there was no guarantee that his heads would vanish if he failed the Maths exam, but he wouldn't know unless he gave it a try.

'Our brave little boy!' Amma gushed. Tanuj had missed only three days of school so there was still a chance to bag that award, she thought.

But now, Appa wasn't sure. 'He shouldn't be going ANYWHERE with ten heads!' he said.

'Of course, he should!' Amma cut in. 'He can stay away from school for a day, a week or even a whole month. But what about after that? Will his heads magically disappear? Should my poor child sit at home all his life and not get out at all?'

No one could stand up against Amma's logic, and so it was decided that Tanuj would go to school.

When the school bus arrived, the driver's eyes popped out. 'You cannot get in wearing that mask!' he grumbled.

'See?' Appa said, as he shrugged and pulled out his scooter key. Soon, he was weaving through the morning traffic with Tanuj firmly seated behind.

Even as passers-by waved and shouted their approval for the innovative Ram-Leela costume (after all, Diwali was just around the corner), Tanuj shut his eyes tight and wished his extra heads would be gone with the wind.

5

At school, Tanuj's classmates were shocked. 'Is it a curse?' 'An evil witch's spell?' they discussed, in hushed tones. They were tempted to tease him but decided to say nothing lest they grew nine heads of their own!

Sushmita Miss stared at him in silence for five whole minutes. School rules said that teachers must not scold students without good reason. Was this a good reason? She was not sure. So, she instructed him to sit on the last row and continued with her lesson.

During lunch break, Tanuj's friends discovered to their delight that each of his heads could simultaneously make a different facial expression. Their excited banter cheered Tanuj up for a while. But when he was made to sit in the stands during football, his heads drooped again.

Over the next few days, Tanuj was the centre of attraction at school. Teachers wanted to click 'selfies' with him, younger students begged for his autograph and the older ones fought to make him part of their 'gang'. Miss Titli, the Drama teacher, was thrilled to bits. Finally, she had the perfect Ravana for the inter-school Ram-Leela competition. Surely, Chunnilal Mehta School would bring back the trophy this year!

And then, Tanuj was invited to meet the Principal himself.

6

The Principal, Mr Khanna, was a shrewd old man. A thin tuft of short grey hair clung to the back of his shiny pate, giving the illusion of a moustache. If you drew a pair of eyes, nose and lips with a marker pen, it would seem like he had two faces – one each on the front and back of his head. It was another matter, of course, that no one dared to draw on the Principal's pate.

'Hmmm,' Mr Khanna said, as he seized Tanuj, examining him from head to toe and side to side. 'So, my boy, how did you manage this extraordinary feat? It is indeed a great day in the history of our school.'

'I don't know, Sir. I wished for them in my dream … I think,' Tanuj mumbled, still wondering how he had grown the extra heads.

'As simple as that, eh? I wish my wishes were granted that easily, then I would be a different man …' said Mr Khanna with a whimsical look, imagining himself as a dashing dude with lush black hair.

But the piercing shriek of the school bell shook him out of his fantasy. 'Uh … hmmm … so, where was I?'

'My heads, Sir. I'm trying all I can, to make them vanish! Until then, I promise I won't cause trouble; I only want to write my exams.'

'No, no, no! Don't wish your heads away, my boy. I'm depending on them to revive the fading glory of our school. Your heads … yes, your fantastic heads, will help get us more admissions.'

Tanuj was puzzled. How could his peculiar problem help the school?

'You must keep the heads together, at least until Diwali break,' Mr Khanna continued. 'That will give ample time for newspapers to be splashed with your photos and ... ahem, mine too ... and ensure that Chunnilal Mehta School is the talk of the town. It won't be long before we attract more and more students to apply for admission for the next academic year.'

'But, Sir ...'

'No buts, my boy,' Mr Khanna's sharp voice cut him short. 'Mind you, your help will not go unappreciated. I'll make special arrangements for you at school. And who knows, you might even win that coveted Best Student Award ...' his voice trailed off.

Tanuj was aghast. To have his photos on the front page of newspapers was awful enough. But being bribed with an award? Horrible! But here was an opportunity to get himself some perks until his heads disappeared. So, picking up a pen and paper from Mr Khanna's desk, he drew up a list of demands.

TANUJ'S LIST

1 Special bus service to and from school

2 To be allowed to skip Assembly at will

3 Extra fans at the last row in class to fan my extra heads

4 Longer lunch hour for me and my best friends, Sunny and Nutty

5 A special toilet that says 'Tanuj's Toilet'

6 No homework for the rest of the year for my whole class

7 Library time instead of PE for me and my friends (see point 4 above) for the whole year

Tanuj went through the list and made some changes. It was too short a time to draw up a complete list, but he was happy he had covered most points. Then, after some thought, he added one more point, just to be on the safe side.

8 I'm not responsible if my heads disappear before the Diwali break. And, if they do disappear, all the above privileges will still hold good.

He then handed the list to the principal, who accepted all the conditions without batting an eyelid. But just as Tanuj turned to leave, Mr Khanna stopped him.

'Ahem ...' he said, clearing his throat. 'While you're still here, there's one more thing you can do for me, my boy.' Then, with a silly grin that went from ear to ear, Mr Khanna produced a smartphone from his trouser pocket and clicked a 'selfie' with Tanuj.

7

The next few days flashed past Tanuj in a blur. Every newspaper in town carried his selfie with Mr Khanna on the front page, and journalists from across the country swarmed outside his house and school.

'Ravana Reborn?' asked the headline of one paper. Yet another newspaper

the daily journal
NEWS TODAY
THE MORNING POST
RAVAN REBORN

asked in bold letters: 'Return of Ravana: Hoax or Reality?'

Tanuj wanted to go into hiding. But then, how would he appear for his exams? After all, the deal with Ravana was to fail in Maths. At first, he felt bad for his parents when he saw them being chased everywhere by the media. But he soon realized that they were enjoying the new-found fame. While Amma bought herself a new Kanjeevaram saree for her TV appearance, Appa went in for a long overdue haircut. So, he stopped feeling guilty and prepared for the exams, making sure not to as much as peep into his Maths books.

On the day of the Maths exam, Tanuj was anxious.

12

8
3
700
2
5
1
7
21+28=49

One glance at each problem, and he knew the method to solve it and get to the right answer. But Ravana's snooping heads stared down at him every time he put his pencil to paper. As he wondered what to do, an idea struck him. He decided to write down all the correct answers. Only, he would jumble them up so that the answer to Problem 1 could be found next to Problem 7, the answer to Problem 2 could be found next to Problem 12 and so on.

'I'm sure Miss Mohanty will understand,' he thought to himself.

Back home, Tanuj's mind was a bundle of mixed feelings. On the one hand, he felt relieved that his extra heads would be gone by the next morning, and on the other, he felt a strange feeling that Appa called 'separation anxiety'. He'd gotten used to his heads and wondered how it would be to go back to his normal self. In an emotional moment, he picked up Appa's phone and clicked a selfie with his parents as a keepsake.

8

A loud 'Ha ha ha' almost startled Tanuj awake as he slept that night. He looked on, with knitted eyebrows, as Ravana rolled around with laughter.

'What is so funny? I hope you're not backing off from your promise …' he asked Ravana, his eyes narrowing to slits. He was in no mood for humour.

'Oh no ... not at all. You have kept your word, my boy, and I too will keep mine. But before that, it is only fair that I get a bit of a laugh.'

Then, closing his eyes, he tried to remember Tanuj's answers. 'Hmmm ... 21+28 = 132. Indeed! I'd love to see the look on your teacher's face as she corrects your paper! What was that second problem? Oh, yes, the number of candies that remained with Anita after distributing some amongst her friends. Any fool would have known the answer is 16, but you wrote 64! And wait, what was your answer to the problem with the clowns' noses? 49, wasn't it? Ho ho ho ... did I have fun watching you write down those hilarious answers!'

‘Okay, okay … you don’t have to rub it in! I’m already feeling miserable that I am going to score 0/30. So, if you’re done laughing, please let me be. And I hope to wake up with just one head tomorrow,’ Tanuj replied, feeling annoyed.

‘Why, of course! Tathastu,’ said Ravana. ‘And since you’ve been such a sport, here’s a secret mantra. If you ever wish to get back your nine heads, all you have to do is chant, “East or West, Ravana is the Best”, three times, before going to bed. But you already know that, don’t you?’ he winked.

'And now, I'll take your leave, or else
Yama will go crazy hunting for me!'
With that, Ravana went POOF! again.

9

When Tanuj woke up the next morning, he felt around for his extra heads. They weren't there. He took a deep breath and peeped into the mirror. Only one head stared back at him.

POOF!

10

Hugging his ‘Best Ravana Award’, Tanuj ran downstairs to give Amma and Appa the good news.

RAVANA TRIVIA

- Ravana was Shiva's greatest devotee. Shiva was so pleased with his devotion that he gifted Ravana his mighty sword – Chandrahas.
- Ravana was so strong, he once lifted the entire Mount Kailasa!
- Ravana was a great scholar and the master of the great books of knowledge – Vedas and Upanishads.
- Ravana was a master of the sciences. He wrote the book 'Ravana Samhita' on astrology, and had knowledge of Ayurveda.
- Ravana was a great musician. While he was an expert Veena player, he is also believed to have invented the instruments Ravanahatha and Rudraveena.
- Ravana was an excellent warrior. He is said to have defeated humans, devas and the serpent races to become the Trilokadipati – Lord of the three worlds.

Ravana was a great king. Under his rule, Lanka was very prosperous and even the poorest of the poor were said to have golden utensils in their houses. No wonder his kingdom was known as 'Sone ki Lanka' (The Golden Lanka)!

But despite these wonderful qualities, the world remembers him as an evil person, because he let his ego tower over all other qualities.

ABOUT THE AUTHOR

Priya Narayanan is a poet and children's author based in Ahmedabad, India. As a child, someone conned her into believing that 'cute' meant 'ugly but bearable'. Since then, she is wary of both the word and that someone! When not practising and teaching design, she likes to read, travel solo and conjure up stories over many cups of coffee and chocolate-chip ice cream. You can learn more about Priya on her website www.priyanarayanan.com

ABOUT THE ILLUSTRATOR

Shamika Chaves is an illustrator and graphic designer based in Mumbai, India. Born into a family of artists, she successfully pursued a degree in applied art and best expresses herself through her illustrations. She enjoys the freedom of hand-rendered illustrations, often using digital media to enhance them. Her work is inspired by the simple joys of everyday life. She lives and works in her cosy little home with her husband, Christopher, and her five-year-old tortoise, Sebastian. Shamika's first book, *Your Journal of Memories*, is being published by HarperCollins India. Visit @shamikasdoodles on Instagram or shamikasdoodles.com to learn more about her work.